For Adam and Rosie

D.L.

For Bryan and Sarah

P.D.

First published 1986 by Walker Books Ltd
87 Vauxhall Walk, London SE11 5HJ

This edition published 1997

2 4 6 8 10 9 7 5 3 1

Printed in Hong Kong

British Library Cataloguing in Publication Data
A catalogue record for this book is available
from the British Library

ISBN 0-7445-5238-9

WRITTEN BY
David Lloyd

ILLUSTRATED BY
Penny Dale

WALKER BOOKS
AND SUBSIDIARIES
LONDON • BOSTON • SYDNEY

Gran said, 'Here's a present, Tom.'

It was a stopwatch.

She started it. Tom stopped it.

It took him 9 seconds.

Tom ran out of his gran's garden.

He ran home in 3 minutes 32 seconds.

He ate his tea in 2 minutes 6 seconds.
His sister Jan said
it was too disgusting to watch.

He got undressed and into the bath and
out again in 1 minute 43 seconds.
Jan said it was cheating not to use soap.

Next morning Tom held his breath
for 32 seconds.

He stood on his head for 11 seconds.

Jan said, ‘Let’s have a staring match.’

Tom lost.

He blinked after 41 seconds.

Then Tom lost his stopwatch.
He searched all over the house.
It took him a long time.
He didn't know how long because
he'd lost the stopwatch.

Jan came in.

She said, 'I can ride my bike to the shop,
eat an ice lolly, meet my friend,
go to the park, climb a tree,
eat another ice lolly and
ride home again in
32 minutes 58 seconds.'

Tom and Jan fought like cat and dog.

Just then Gran arrived.
She said, ‘Stop that fighting!
Stop it at once!’

‘Guess what, Gran,’ Tom said.

'We just fought for exactly 7 minutes.'

MORE WALKER PAPERBACKS
For You to Enjoy

HELLO, GOODBYE
by David Lloyd/Louise Voce

First there is just a tree. Then a bear comes along, then a bee, then all sorts of other animals appear – and disappear!

"Wonderful story... Bright, simple illustrations... A good book to use as a reading aid and great for the young child, too."
Nursery World

0-7445-1348-0 £3.99

TEN IN THE BED
by Penny Dale

"A subtle variation on the traditional nursery song, illustrated with wonderfully warm pictures ... crammed with amusing details." *Practical Parenting*

0-7445-1340-5 £4.50

BET YOU CAN'T!
by Penny Dale

"A lively argumentative dialogue – using simple, repetitive words – between two children. Illustrated with great humour and realism." *Practical Parenting*

0-7445-1225-5 £3.99